Field Day
A lesson on empathy

by Suzanne I. Barchers
illustrated by Mattia Cerato

RED CHAIR PRESS

Please visit our website at **www.redchairpress.com**.
Find a free catalog of all our high-quality products for young readers.

Field Day

Library of Congress Control Number: 2011934547
ISBN: 978-1-937529-01-7 (pbk)
ISBN: 978-1-937529-09-3 (hc)

Lexile is a registered trademark of MetaMetrics, Inc. Used with permission.
Leveling provided by Linda Cornwell of Literacy Connections Consulting.

This edition first published in 2012 by
Red Chair Press, LLC   PO Box 333   South Egremont, MA 01258-0333

Printed in China
1 2 3 4 5 16 15 14 13 12

Bun

Pip

Sox

Tab

Ted

Field Day

The five friends are happy about Field Day and the fun they will have. But then they learn that there is no race for turtles! Can the friends come up with a plan to help their pal Peter have fun too?

"Hooray!" says Pip. "It's finally here!

It's Field Day at last, the best day of the year."

"I've entered the tree jump," Pip says with a shake.

"I think I can win if no branches break."

"I'm doing the long hop," Bun says with a twitch.

"We're hopping across a very wide ditch."

"I'm doing the dash," Tab says with a grin.

"Chasing the field mice might help me win."

"The speed roll's my race," Ted says with a wiggle.

"I can roll really fast if my quills do not jiggle."

"I've entered the fun run," Sox says to Peter.

"I hope I can win since it's only one meter."

"I wish I could race," Peter says with a frown.

"There's no race for turtles. We'd all slow it down."

"But I'll still have fun. I'll watch you from here.

You do your best. I'll clap and I'll cheer!"

Bun looks at her pals as she raises her eyes.

"There's no race for turtles? What a surprise!"

The pals talk together. They decide what to do.

They plan a fun race that Peter can do too.

The pals watch the turtles slide in their race.

They all clap and cheer as Peter wins first place!

Big Questions:

Are the five friends happy that it is Field Day? Look on pages 16-17. How do you know Peter is sad?

Was Peter happy at the end of the story? How did the friends solve Peter's problem?

Big Words:

decide: agree on something

meter: a unit of length or distance

race: a contest to see who is fastest on a course

Discuss

➥ Peter was sad there was no race for turtles. Have you ever felt left out of an activity others were playing? Think of two words to describe how you felt.

➥ The friends made up a race for turtles: to slide down a hill on their shells. What kind of race would be your favorite?

Activity

➥ Act out the kinds of races in the story as the different friends might do them.

tree jump   long hop   dash
fun run   speed roll

➥ Think about a talent you have. Maybe you like to draw or play soccer. Draw a picture of yourself with a First Place ribbon.

About the Author

Suzanne I. Barchers, Ed.D., began a career in writing and publishing after fifteen years as a teacher. She has written over 100 children's books, two college textbooks, and more than 20 reader's theater and teacher resource books. She previously held editorial roles at Weekly Reader and LeapFrog and is on the PBS Kids Media Advisory Board for the next generation of children's programming. Suzanne also plays the flute professionally—and for fun—from her home in Stanford, CA.

About the Illustrator

Mattia Cerato was born in Cuneo, a small town in northern Italy where he still lives and works. As soon as he could hold a pencil he loved sketching things he saw around him. When he is not drawing, Mattia loves traveling around the world, reading good books, and playing and listening to cool music.

 For a free activity page for this story, go to www.redchairpress.com and look for Free Activities.